HERMAN

THE DINOSAUR

BOOK ONE

SHARON M. COOPER

PAGE PUBLISHING
Conneaut Lake, PA

First originally published by Page Publishing 2022

ISBN 979-8-88654-287-5 (pbk)
ISBN 979-8-88654-288-2 (digital)

Printed in the United States of America

Dedication

I would like to thank my parents, Carlton
and Nellie, for their encouragement.

I would like to dedicate this book
to my borrowed children:
Emma, Amitay, Orian, and Micah.

It was a cold, sunny morning. Herman's mom has just made breakfast for him, and he wanted to go for a walk in the woods with his older brother, Colin.

Herman and Colin walked down a path filled with trees that were shedding for the fall. He picked up a leaf and looked at the many colors in it. Herman wondered how can so many colors could be on one leaf.

He started sighing. Today, Herman was having his first playdate, and he was nervous. He was thinking of what to bring to the boy that he was meeting today. Herman thought to himself, *What if the boy doesn't like what I like*? Colin noticed that Herman was bothered about something.

"Hey, Herman," said Colin, "are you thinking about your playdate? I bet you are wondering what to bring and what to do. Why don't you bring some of those leaves, and you can make a picture out of it? I used to do that when I was your age."

Herman brightened up and said, "That's a great idea! Maybe we can glue the leaves on a paper!"

"You got an excellent idea, Herman, let's collect the leaves," said Colin.

After collecting the leaves, Colin said, "Come on, Herman, we must get back home, or you will be late for your first playdate!" The brothers quickly hurried back to their house.

Herman's mom, Caroline, was driving him to the playdate. Herman sat in the back seat, looked up at the sunroof, and then started looking out of the window, his eyes wide with wonder. Herman was amazed at the new town he was heading into.

They were heading to a playdate at Herman's mother's friend's house. Herman kept thinking how to make friends on a playdate. "Who is this kid anyway?" Herman asked his mom.

"He is Johann, the son of my friend, Millie, from work. Herman, you're going to like him. I met him when I dropped off his mom yesterday on our way home from work. Johann just got home from preschool and looked bored. He was glad to see his mom, but he wanted to play with someone."

When they arrived at the house, Herman saw Johann sitting on the front steps. Herman's eyes opened wide. He noticed that Johann was holding a box in his hands. Herman's mom, helping him get out of the car, told him, "Herman, now everything will be just fine. Meeting other children on playdates can help you to make good friends." Herman slowly got out of the car and started walking toward the house with

his mother. Johann, who was sitting on the front steps, noticed that Herman had a box in his hands. Herman had put the leaves in a plastic baggy in the box, and Herman's mom had made chocolate chip cookies and wanted to surprise them. So she placed the cookies in a container inside the box.

Johann's mother, Millie, stepped from the front door to greet Herman and his mom. "Hi, Caroline and Herman, I'm glad you two came!" said Millie.

"Hi, Millie, thank you so much for having us over!" said Caroline.

"Come on inside, Caroline and Herman. Johann, why don't you take Herman to the playroom?"

"Can I show Herman around the house first, Mom?" asked Johann.

"Of course!" said Johann's mom.

Johann said, "Come on, let's play!"

But Herman said, "No way!"

"Aw, Herman," said his mother, kneeing down and whispering to him, "You won't know if you like it unless you try it."

"Aw, okay, Mom," Herman whispered to her. "I'll try."

"Don't forget about the leaves and cookies," said Herman's mom.

They went into the living room. "I want to show you my cat, Alastair," said Johann. Alistair sat on one of the chairs, licking his paws and washing his face. Alastair meowed at the boys and jumped off the chair, rubbing their legs as he went along.

Johann showed Herman the house from top to bottom, ending up in the playroom.

In the playroom, Johann placed his box on a table and opened it. It was a book of shapes that you could cut out to make different objects. Herman's eyes opened with surprise! "Oh wow," Herman said. "That's so cool!"

Johann laughed, saying, "All of my friends say the same thing."

Herman asked Johann, "You have friends?"

"I just started making friends," Johann said. "I had a few playdates."

Herman then opened his box and took out the bag of leaves and the cookie container. Johann saw the leaves and said, "Wow, what awesome colors! Maybe we can make a picture and glue the leaves on? I have glue, paper, crayons, and markers."

"Yeah!" said Herman excitedly. "I have chocolate chip cookies. Do you like them?" asked Herman.

"I love chocolate chip cookies—they are my favorite!" said Johann.

Johann and Herman made cars out of the shapes and then made a picture. They drew a road and glued the cars on it. They then drew trees and then glued the leaves to the trees.

Johann's mom, Millie, came to the playroom door and said, "Snack time, boys." Herman gave the cookie box to Johann, and the boys went into the kitchen and saw a table full of food. Sitting at the dining room table, their moms were having tea and coffee. There were strawberries, blueberries, chicken fingers, bow tie pasta, water and apple juice.

"Aw, strawberries—I love strawberries!" said Herman. "They are my favorite fruit."

"I like the blueberries. My mom and I made blueberry pie. There's some left over if you want to try it for dessert," said Johann.

"Don't forget my chocolate chip cookies," said Herman.

Herman's mother called from the door, "Herman, it's time to go home. Say goodbye to Johann and tell him thank you for having me over."

Herman said, "Thank you, Johann, for having me, but I don't want to leave now."

"You can come back, or maybe better, can I come to your house?" asked Johann.

"I'll ask my mom," said Herman, but Herman's mom already figured that Johann would want to come to their house and said, "Herman, I invited them to our house next week!"

Millie and Johann walked Herman and his mom outside to the driveway. Caroline and Millie hugged and said, "See you at work on Monday!" The boys gave each other a high five. Herman's mom helped him into their car, and the sun started to set as they were driving away.

"Mom, I had such an awesome time—I really like playdates!" said Herman.

"I am glad you enjoyed playing with someone new, but I am gladder that you gave it a try. I am very proud of you, Herman," said his mom.

When Herman and his mom got home, Herman ran to Colin, holding something behind his back and told him what a great time they had. "Did you make the picture with the leaves?" asked Colin. Herman then showed his brother the picture that he was holding behind his back.

"Yes, and I told Johann that I wanted to give the picture to you," said Herman.

"Aw, Herman, that is so thoughtful of you—thanks, bro!" said Colin.

"You are awesome welcome!" said Herman. The boys then went into the backyard to play before dinner.

The End.

About the Author

Having a lot of passion and knowledge working with children, Sharon M. Cooper has experienced the many things that children go through growing up. She is excited to publish her first book about a first playdate. She currently works as a nanny and lives in New Jersey with her energetic cat, Salem, who thinks he's human!